er
bitats

Beaches

JoAnn Early Macken

Reading consultant: Susan Nations, M. Ed.,
author, literacy coach, consultant

WR WEEKLY
READER
EARLY LEARNING LIBRARY

Please visit our web site at: www.earlyliteracy.cc
For a free color catalog describing Weekly Reader® Early Learning Library's list
of high-quality books, call 1-877-445-5824 (USA) or 1-800-387-3178 (Canada).
Weekly Reader® Early Learning Library's fax: (414) 336-0164.

Library of Congress Cataloging-in-Publication Data

Macken, JoAnn Early, 1953-
    Beaches / JoAnn Early Macken.
       p. cm. — (Water habitats)
    Includes bibliographical references and index.
    ISBN 0-8368-4882-9 (lib. bdg.)
    ISBN 0-8368-4889-6 (softcover)
    1. Seashore ecology—Juvenile literature. 2. Beaches—Juvenile
literature. I. Title.
    QH541.5.S35M33   2005
    578.769'9—dc22   2005043986

This edition first published in 2006 by
Weekly Reader® Early Learning Library
A Member of the WRC Media Family of Companies
330 West Olive Street, Suite 100
Milwaukee, WI 53212 USA

Art direction: Tammy West
Cover design and page layout: Kami Koenig
Picture research: Diane Laska-Swanke

Picture credits: Cover, © Reinhard Dirscherl/SeaPics.com; p. 5 © Jon Cornforth/SeaPics.com;
p. 7 © Niall Benvie/naturepl.com; pp. 9, 15 © Tom and Pat Leeson; p. 11 © Graeme Teague;
p. 13 © Joe McDonald/Visuals Unlimited; p. 17 © Robert F. Myers/Visuals Unlimited;
p. 19 © Alan & Sandy Carey; p. 21 © Doug Perrine/SeaPics.com

Printed in the United States of America

1 2 3 4 5 6 7 8 9 09 08 07 06 05

Note to Educators and Parents

Reading is such an exciting adventure for young children! They are beginning to integrate their oral language skills with written language. To encourage children along the path to early literacy, books must be colorful, engaging, and interesting; they should invite the young reader to explore both the print and the pictures.

Water Habitats is a new series designed to help children read about the plants and animals that thrive in and around water. Each book describes a different watery environment and some of its resident wildlife.

Each book is specially designed to support the young reader in the reading process. The familiar topics are appealing to young children and invite them to read — and reread — again and again. The full-color photographs and enhanced text further support the student during the reading process.

In addition to serving as wonderful picture books in schools, libraries, homes, and other places where children learn to love reading, these books are specifically intended to be read within an instructional guided reading group. This small group setting allows beginning readers to work with a fluent adult model as they make meaning from the text. After children develop fluency with the text and content, the book can be read independently. Children and adults alike will find these books supportive, engaging, and fun!

— Susan Nations, M.Ed., author, literacy coach,
and consultant in literacy development

On a beach, waves wash onto stones or sand. The wind pushes sand into piles. Piles of sand are called **dunes**.

Wind and waves can break down rocks. Rocks break into sand. Sand can also be bits of shell and coral.

shells

7

Clams dig down into the sand. Shells protect their soft bodies.

Grass grows in the sand.
Insects and small animals
hide in the grass.

Birds with long legs run from the waves. They poke their bills into the sand. Birds eat insects, crabs, and worms.

13

Barnacles stick to rocks on the beach. They wait for waves to wash in. Waves bring them food to eat.

barnacles

15

A hermit crab lives in an old snail shell. When the crab grows too large, it finds a new home.

shell

Gulls fly high above the beach. They fly in circles over the beach. One gull catches a fish.

Baby turtles hatch from eggs in the sand. They cross the beach at night to find water. They swim off into the ocean.

Glossary

barnacles — water animals with shells made of plates. Barnacles attach to rocks or other animals.

bills — beaks

clams — water animals whose shells have two parts that open and close

hatch — to break out of an egg

sand — tiny pieces of rock, shell, or coral

snail — a slow-moving water animal with a shell that forms a spiral

For More Information

Books

A House for Hermit Crab. Eric Carle (Aladdin)

I Live Near the Ocean. Where I Live (series). Gini Holland
  (Weekly Reader Early Learning Library)

The Tide. Nik Pollard (Roaring Brook Press)

Where Land Meets Sea. Rookie Read-About Science (series).
  Allan Fowler (Children's Press)

Web Site

Sea Turtles
*www.npca.org/marine_and_coastal/marine_wildlife/
  seaturtles.asp*
Different types of sea turtles and where they live

Index

About the Author

JoAnn Early Macken is the author of two rhyming picture books, *Sing-Along Song* and *Cats on Judy*, and many other nonfiction books for beginning readers. Her poems have appeared in several children's magazines. A graduate of the M.F.A. in Writing for Children and Young Adults program at Vermont College, she lives in Wisconsin with her husband and their two sons. Visit her Web site at www.joannmacken.com.

24